S0-CJM-011

Robert "Jungle Bob" Smith was born in Manhattan but spent his youth on Long Island where he was introduced to and developed a fondness for reptiles and amphibians.

A lifelong passion to learn more about these fascinating creatures ensued. He is a devout traveler with over 50 trips to exotic locations around the globe. He owned and bred well over 100 species. He is well versed on both the captive husbandry and natural history of reptiles, but his greatest talent is his ability to communicate to all ages and impart his knowledge about the subject to all.

Jungle Bob is a much sought-after public speaker, a regular on local New York television and popular on You Tube. Whatever he does professionally however the goal remains the same: raise the public's perception about these unusual animals in an effort to better understand their role in nature. There are as many myths and misconceptions as there are facts circulating about them that they are sometimes referred to as the Unloved members of the animal kingdom.

Lenny is Jungle Bobs first in a series of children's books. Like all good fables there is a moral to the story, but it also educates the reader by weaving incredible facts about the main character, a legless lizard, who suffers from "being different". Lenny is teased and bullied only to find his differences actually make him better!

Through his company Jungle Bob Enterprises, Jungle Bob runs reptile only pet stores, produces reptile and aquarium products, lectures at schools, nature centers and libraries and still finds time to tromp around rainforests and deserts in search of the truth about exotic animals.

About the Artist

Steve Sabella is a renowned artist whose accomplishments include, album covers, pet product design, comic books and cartoons.
When he is not dazzling readers with his incredible artwork and imagination, he is managing a store at Jungle Bobs Reptile World.

Lenny…A Most Unusual Reptile

Copyright © 2019 by Jungle Bob Enterprises, Inc.

All rights reserved. No part of this book may be reproduced or transmitted in any form or by any means without written permission from the author.

ISBN (978-0-578-22375-9)

Printed in USA

LENNY HUNG AROUND WITH A BUNCH OF FRIENDS WHO WERE GARTER SNAKES

THEY WERE NOT ALWAYS NICE TO LENNY!

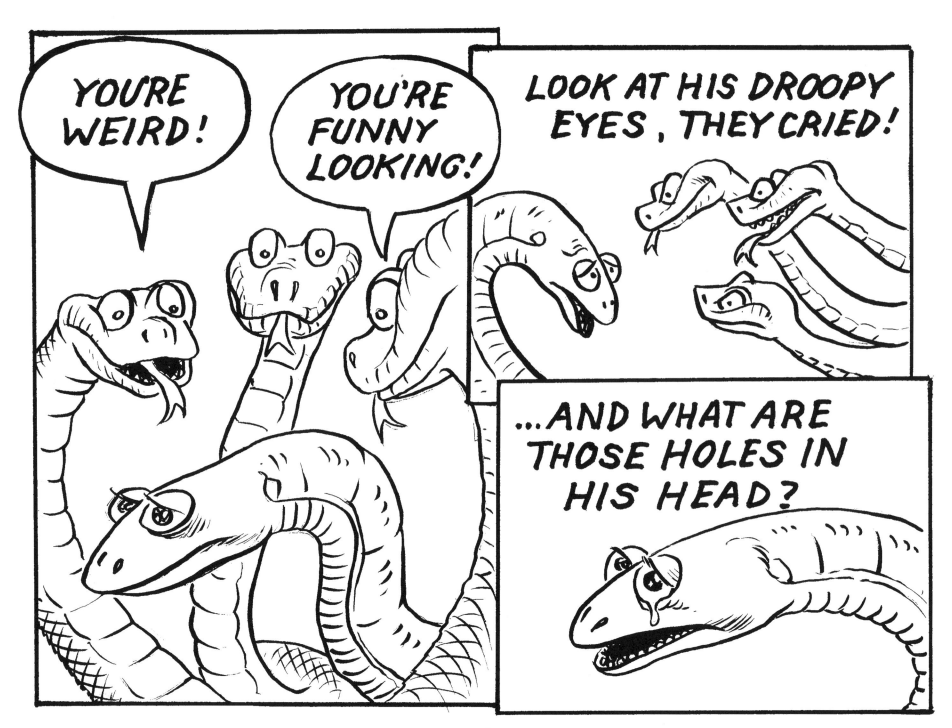

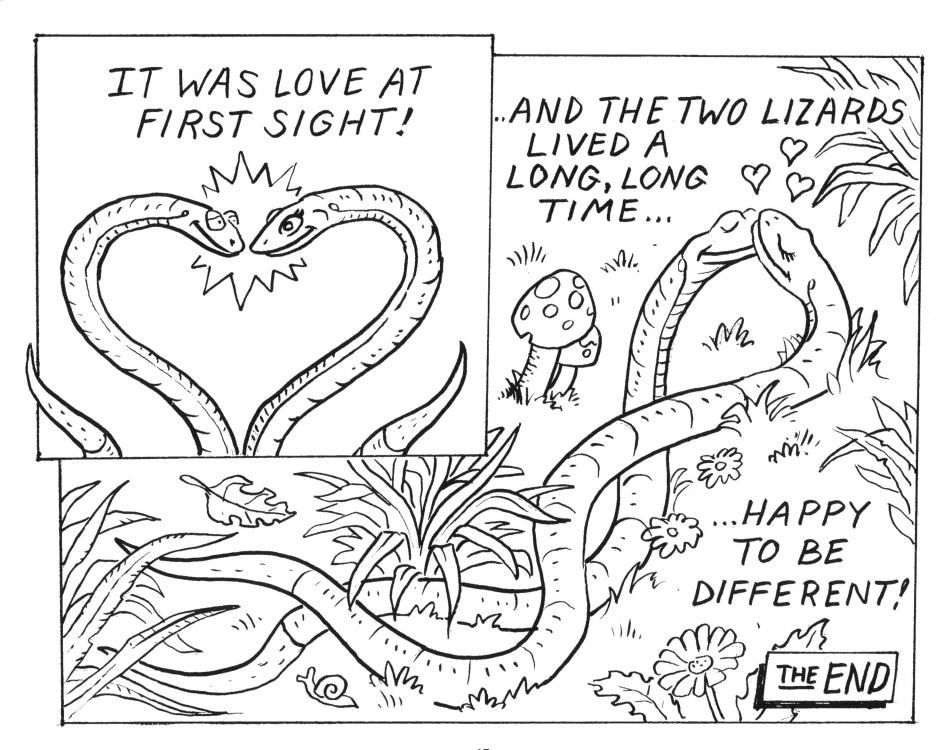

FUN FACTS

- Legless lizards can detach their tails! Called Autotomy as it is a reflex action that separates their body from their tail allowing them to escape predators.
- The broken tail will grow back! But never as perfect as the original.
- They are so unusual they have many names including Glass Lizard, Slow Worm and in Eastern Europe Legless Lizards are known as "Sheltopusiks"!
- Sheltopusiks can live over 30 years in captivity!
- Legless lizards are carnivores and eat a wide variety of food from rodents to insects.
- There are many species and can be found in North America, Europe, Asia and Australia.

Notes to Parents and Teachers

Helping children feel good about their individuality is critical to counteract bullying. Bullying comes in various forms including teasing, name-calling, taunting or embarrassing someone in public.

The main character in this story, Lenny, is made fun of for being different. In the end, his differences are what keep him alive to live happily ever after.

It is the hope of the author that through Lenny's story, children will recognize and be encouraged to tolerate differences. Understanding that Lenny the Lizard's differences are a biological FACT, may increase their sense of natural wonder prompting them to turn off their devices and GO EXPLORE THE GREAT OUTDOORS!!

Suggested questions for child/student after reading the book:

1. How did Lenny feel when the other animals made fun of him?
2. What are some of the things the other animals said to him?
3. Was Lenny nice to the other animals?
4. How did Lenny help them?
5. Why did the snakes not hear Lenny's warnings?
6. What parts of Lenny's body saved him?
7. So... what actually is the difference between a Lizard and a Snake?

Vocabulary

1. Reptile
2. Predators
3. Captivity
4. Carnivore